Grim 101

Book 1

Artist / Author: T. Davies
www.teddaviesartistry.com

Campaign mgtm: Lisa Melone
lisaleemelone@gmail.com

Editor: Brian K. Morris
bkmorris56@gmail.com

Book Layouts: Caitlin Ryan
lintastic.editor@gmail.com

Grim 101 book1 August 2021. Published by Ted Davies & Grim101 copyright of Ted Davies. All rights reserve. All characters, events, and institutions depicted herein are fictional. All similarities are unintended and coincidental. No reproduction without written consent from Ted Davies, creator of Grim 101 book1 and series.

Grim 101

Preface:

I have always been enchanted by relic architecture, ruins in any form and forgotten graveyards. My fascination with the last of this eclectic list started when I was a young boy.

Being the youngest of 43 grandchildren I was surrounded by death.

Yearly, it seemed, the funerals were as consistent as birthdays. My mother, being the youngest child in a rural farming family of 15 children, would always have a relation "moving on" as they would say. So, going to a funeral and a burial in a cemetery was a seemingly natural way to spend my years growing up.

When I was about 12 years of age, I wondered why I always felt anxious or sad when I entered a cemetery for another one of these "events." Due to the large age difference between my mother's siblings, half of the aunts, uncles, cousins, whatever, I never knew them. So, why was I feeling this way? Was it grief or guilt? How could it be if I didn't even know these people from Adam?

That's when I had this thought for the first time: What if, it wasn't me? What if it was a someone or something whose job it was to make us feel this way? And as I grew up,

I wondered if it hated its' job and what if it wasn't particularly good at it? How alone would it feel and could a change in occupation even be an option? Or maybe, it had a great sense of humor, but no one could hear the punchlines? This is what started my journey of "Grim 101" and the story of "Jim" the cemetery Grim. Please enjoy this memoir style dark romantic comedy series and maybe smile the next time you pass by an old forgotten cemetery...

Author: J. Davies

Dedicated to Christine, my muse, and my inspirations Ashley and Aaron.

I was invisible, until she saw me... No, really. I have been floating around this cemetery for years. I guess my origins, as it were, should be my start to this tale. Unfortunately, I recall only this place, and from where I come from, well, that was anyone's guess. This relic of a book was a cruel guide. "Grim 101," what a terrible title for such a dreadful manual of despair. I cannot believe that I would have taken such a supernatural vocation. But a duty was a mistress in this solitude, of eternal watching. I have been a mere observer, at best, for more than 150 years. Jim

"Beginings"

I should place in this memoir a beginning or at least a starting point of my experience here. I do not believe these words I tell you now any more than you do reading them. But I promise to build my truth for you, in every recollection. So that you may understand my burden and unique "perspective."

My days have been many here, weaving a tapestry of lost moments. I have written this memoir so I too can remember. For my burden of time in this exile has taught me many things but has never gifted to me a lost memory. These written words may grant me a reference from where I can exist or at least find some humor in all of this.

"The Book"

I found myself many, many years ago, here, floating, I say about 20 feet off the cemetery ground. I awakened when the tails of this old coat were tangled in the branches of a tall oak tree. It had made enough fuss for me to regain my senses. Unfortunately, this was all I regained because from that point I remembered nothing prior to my time here. Once I was awake, I grabbed that tall oak tree almost from instinct. I thought I was falling, but, here, strangely, I floated. Securing myself to a large branch I looked down toward the cemetery floor and saw, amidst a sea of grey and weathered gravestones an old, worn, red leathered book. I saw an inscription, but I needed to get closer to fully read it. So, I made my way down the tree to the mossy ground, all the while, floating, as an awkward feather in a brisk wind. Finally, I made it to the book and read its cover, "Grim 101."

I took the relic in hand to discover that a fiery, pain overtook my foot and leg the closer I placed myself to the hallowed ground. However, I was more interested in the book than of my discomfort. It may have answers to my current situation. To mind, a memory lost, of who, what, where, when & why I am here.

My days of reading this manual's contents have been many. But alas, I never caused a whimper or grieving wail from anyone not already in the throes of mourning. On the contrary, I made many grief-stricken visitors more at ease, even giddy. Some, over the years, have been so tickled that they have laughed out loud. Could you imagine any laughter in such a dismal place? But there it was, enjoyment in my gated exile. The "living", would even enjoy picnics with their deceased. Not Physically, of course, but beside the gravestones, as if the person they mourned was at the head of some sort of outdoor table. Angst and anxiety were not mine to give as the "Grim 101" spelled out.

"Rules"

Investigating the book, I discovered that it was a manual of how to be a "Grim" of a cemetery. A "Grim" as described in this book was a "being with the charge and authority to make all the living feel despair, anxiety and all forms of hopelessness."

Opening this old text, I read its pages. There were three very direct rules, and I prayed they were guidelines. The heading of the first page stated:

Rules of a Cemetery Grim

1. Cause grief and despair on all living that visit the cemetery grounds.

2. Cause anxiety and hopelessness on all living that visit the cemetery grounds.

3. Cause a complete experience of dread in all living that visit the cemetery grounds.

It spelled out how to make it an uncomfortable event for the visiting living, I am not made for that, I love to laugh and share a funny story or two. It was the farthest from who I believe I am.

"Roots"

The trees brought to me envy. I have become jealous of them. Their family, rooted, intwined, always connected. Subjecting and shading me with their privilege. Yet they have been my only companions in this place, ironically, my roots...

They, my timekeepers, my calendars, sometimes even my perches. These saplings turned stoics have given me an aerial viewpoint and a perspective since I awoke here.

Their leaves, the lost memories of seasons enjoyed once, like my memories, fallen away. Taken by autumn's wind, not knowing their origin or their destination.

"Pretending"

I have often wondered if I was buried amongst these graves. Or I was mourned in another part of this world? Sometimes when a small group of "the living" enter these old gates, I imagine they might be paying their respects or mourning me. Always, the silent imposter, wondering if it were my loved ones at my gravesite. My widow, daughter or sister, grieving the remarkable man I once was but cannot remember.

Twisted, but there it was, my quiet, invisible existence played tricks with my sanity...

"Escape"

I have tried to leave these gates. I even attempted to walk on these grounds. Knowing the agony, it caused, I still strove for freedom.

Why is it that when burdens become habitual, we are lost to them? We forget it can be different and we just accept our lot.

I am not there...

Sometimes we need to lie to ourselves to see even a small part of the truth. My truth is eternity. How long do I continue lying to myself?

"Dilemma"

I still wonder if I am dead. I existed, trapped in a forgotten place. Why was I unseen and unheard? Am I the forgotten, the unremembered, the lost? Who mourned me, or was I ever alive to be mourned? Now, my dilemma is presented to you.

Sometimes even the dead could be seen in a vapor or out of the corner of the living's eye. For some reason, I lacked such a charity as the observer of this garden.

"Smallest Stones"

I have witnessed many a sadness for the ones grieving. But I believe I have experienced none more sorrowful as a child's passing. The anguish of the parents, I have felt to my core within these gates. It truly is the saddest I can recall feeling. These small beings were loved the most and grieving was not the process for the loss of these little ones. It had no name or timeline; it was complete sorrow in the purest of heartbreaking form. The smallest stones were the markers of these tiny angels. I have shed many tears for these children and their families. For their loved *ones, remaining, no sanctuary was given and no burden heavier.*

"Tick Tock"

Time is not a burden of the dead and eternity does not employ timekeepers. The sunrises and sunsets are my sundial of sorts which manage my blistering schedule. I often say this in jest to myself, remembering this memoir is to aid in my recall of my days.

Pondering my moments in this exile I have realized one thing: Silence is not always golden. It can be deafening and painfully singular. Small amounts of time can extend to unwanted lengths here.

"Curious"

As time passed, life and its distractions have moved more and more of the living away, leaving ruins of forgotten lifetimes overgrown with moss. I have witnessed every so often a curious living soul finding their way into my surroundings. They usually tried to read worn stone markers with their sad scribbles of names and dates weathered smooth, almost erasing the memory of the grave's occupant. These visitors searched for clues but soon lost interest when engravings are too hard to decipher.

Many of the living would get bored easily. The task of inquiry would move them only so far. I have seen one that appreciated the discovery of the past that surrounded them.

She intrigued me...

"Intruder?"

I first noticed her at the old cottage just outside the cemetery walls. She had freed the rusted iron gate from its age. It grew orange from neglect but remained solid and secure. She did so with a reverence, a respect, to the sacredness of this place. Stepping thoughtfully around my still garden. Admiring every grave as she carefully investigated my overgrown sanctuary. She gripped my attention as an icy morning held the frozen dew.

Her distraction, although welcome, confused me. It magnified my feelings of concern.

Why my silent invisible eternity in this place?

"Juniper"

I watch her from afar, but I have to say I admire her when she is closer. I never saw such a striking color of auburn hair, not to mention her alabaster white skin and piercing sea green eyes. The air smells of juniper when she walks by me. She haunts me.

Her clothing looks as if she is a gypsy. A menagerie of many colors and fabrics made into her shawls and dresses. I have seen her wear very peculiar outfits when tending her garden. Surprising the sun does not leave its mark on her skin where exposed. She makes my eternity *tolerable and unbearable in the same moment.*

"Hello there"

My burden has been lifted today. I felt miracles were possible, but I have not witnessed one until now. She woke early this morning and as usual took to tending her garden outside the old cottage. Juniper filled the air, and I was again captured. Weeding and watering her herbs and flowers, she suddenly stopped. Concerned for safety, she looked around quickly. Her eyes locked to the gravestone that I had been perched on. I know she could not hear me, but I silently sat there not moving an inch.

Reaching into the pocket of her dress, she pulled out a small stone. This stone was unremarkable except for a hole that went directly through its center. It looked like a decorative piece to be worn on a string around the neck. Raising the stone to her eye, she peered through it, moving toward my position. All the while, squinting one eye with her mouth slightly in smile, searching for her hidden stalker...

She locked her gaze and said, still smiling, the kindest words I have ever heard.

"Hello there! I see you, I'm Gwen..."

Thank You to the Backers!!!

Brandon Eaker
Peter Ryan
Billy Tucci and Crusade Fine Arts, Ltd.
Eric Cacioppo
Grant Lankard
Lisa Boyd
Captain Action
Travis Gibb
Mary Gaitan
Suzanne
Wren
STTX
Amy Williams Mott
Chuck Pineau
Brian K. Morris
Eric J. Sorlien
Nuncuncoo1
Rebecca
Lacie Swick

Four Corners Collectables	Duwang
Jairred Lambert	Dan Schouest
Louis Bright-Raven	Jeff Hayes
Karl Witsman	Lisa Melone
Brian Rodman	Chris
Paul Massaro	Stefani Menard
Natasha Mathisrud	Gerald Schroder
Aaron Dowen	SeerNova Comics
Dan Hollifield	Gary Phillips
Eric Hawkins	Kathryn Nevill
Sean Gatcomb	Candice Grundy
Midknight42	Onrie Kompan
Avary Powell	Arman Nasim
Mihai	Keisha Acuff
Ken Leinaar	Willow Skylor
Chickadee	Janette
Russell Allen	The Creative Fund by
Kim Borland	Backer Kit
Heather Ellen	All of Ted's Tribe
Tobey Zehr	

Other Works from Ted Davies

www.teddaviesartistry.com